HOPSCOTCH
TWISTY TALES

The Lovely Duckling

by Penny Dolan and David Boyle

This story is based on the traditional fairy tale,
The Ugly Duckling, but with a new twist.
You can read the original story in
Hopscotch Fairy Tales. Can you make
up your own twist for the story?

First published in 2013 by
Franklin Watts
338 Euston Road
London
NW1 3BH

Franklin Watts Australia
Level 17/207 Kent Street
Sydney
NSW 2000

Text © Penny Dolan 2013
Illustrations © David Boyle 2013

A CIP catalogue record for this book is available
from the British Library.

ISBN 978 1 4451 1627 3 (hbk)
ISBN 978 1 4451 1633 4 (pbk)

Series Editor: Melanie Palmer
Series Advisor: Catherine Glavina
Series Designer: Peter Scoulding

Printed in China

Franklin Watts is a division of
Hachette Children's Books,
an Hachette UK company
www.hachette.co.uk

Down by the pond sat Mother Duck.
She was very proud of the four
blue eggs in her nest.

Crack! The first egg hatched.
Out of the shell came a large
duckling. His stubby wings had
very dark feathers.

"Oh dear," quacked the other ducks. "He's not very lovely."

Crack! The second duckling hatched. Her feet were a bit too big.

"Oh dear," quacked the nosy ducks. "She looks clumsy."

Peck! Peck! The third duckling poked her way out of her shell. "Oh dear," the ducks quacked. "What a big beak."

Now there was only one egg left in the nest. Nobody said a word.

At long last, the egg hatched.
Out popped a bundle of fluff.
"Now that," sighed the ducks,
"is a perfect duckling."

The fourth duckling had a pretty yellow beak and neat yellow feet. Her feathers were as soft and fluffy as thistledown.

"I will call her Beauty," said
Mother Duck proudly.
All the animals in the farmyard
came to see the lovely duckling.

"Beauty," said Mother Duck, "From now on you must look your best at all times."

She made Beauty sit in the
nest while the others paddled
in the river.

Mother Duck fluffed up Beauty's feathers six times a day.
Beauty was very proud.

"Look at me! Aren't I the loveliest duckling?" she said. Beauty turned up her beak at the other ducklings.

Soon everyone got bored
with admiring Beauty.
She was left all alone.

Meanwhile, the first duckling spread his wings and tried to fly.

The second duckling paddled her
feet so hard she swam faster than
any of the other ducks.

The third duckling poked her beak down among the cool green weeds and found plenty of food.

Beauty began to feel sorry for herself. The other ducklings were having so much fun. She began to cry.

"Come and join us, you silly duck," the other ducklings called. Beauty did not wait to ask Mother Duck.

She darted out of the nest and
into the water.

"Hooray!" quacked the ducklings.

"Hooray!" quacked Beauty.

Beauty wasn't ever the fastest flier
or the best swimmer or the
cleverest diver.

But she learned to have lots of fun
and make friends – and that was
good enough for the little duck.

Puzzle 1

Put these pictures in the correct order.
Which event do you think is most important?
Now try writing the story in your own words!

Puzzle 2

Choose the correct speech bubbles for each character. Can you think of any others? Turn over to find the answers.

Answers

Puzzle 1

The correct order is: 1c, 2f, 3e, 4a, 5d, 6b

Puzzle 2

Beauty: 3, 5

The other ducklings: 1, 4

Mother Duck: 2, 6

Look out for more Hopscotch Twisty Tales and Fairy Tales:

TWISTY TALES
The Lovely Duckling
ISBN 978 1 4451 1627 3*
ISBN 978 1 4451 1633 4
Hansel and Gretel and the Green Witch
ISBN 978 1 4451 1628 0*
ISBN 978 1 4451 1634 1
The Emperor's New Kit
ISBN 978 1 4451 1629 7*
ISBN 978 1 4451 1635 8
Rapunzel and the Prince of Pop
ISBN 978 1 4451 1630 3*
ISBN 978 1 4451 1636 5
Dick Whittington Gets on his Bike
ISBN 978 1 4451 1631 0*
ISBN 978 1 4451 1637 2
The Pied Piper and the Wrong Song
ISBN 978 1 4451 1632 7*
ISBN 978 1 4451 1638 9
The Princess and the Frozen Peas
ISBN 978 1 4451 0675 5
Snow White Sees the Light
ISBN 978 1 4451 0676 2

The Elves and the Trendy Shoes
ISBN 978 1 4451 0678 6
The Three Frilly Goats Fluff
ISBN 978 1 4451 0677 9
Princess Frog
ISBN 978 1 4451 0679 3
Rumpled Stilton Skin
ISBN 978 1 4451 0680 9
Jack and the Bean Pie
ISBN 978 1 4451 0182 8
Brownilocks and the Three Bowls of Cornflakes
ISBN 978 1 4451 0183 5
Cinderella's Big Foot
ISBN 978 1 4451 0184 2
Little Bad Riding Hood
ISBN 978 1 4451 0185 9
Sleeping Beauty – 100 Years Later
ISBN 978 1 4451 0186 6

FAIRY TALES
The Three Little Pigs
ISBN 978 0 7496 7905 7
Little Red Riding Hood
ISBN 978 0 7496 7907 1
Goldilocks and the Three Bears
ISBN 978 0 7496 7903 3
Hansel and Gretel
ISBN 978 0 7496 7904 0

Rapunzel
ISBN 978 0 7496 7906 4
Rumpelstiltskin
ISBN 978 0 7496 7908 8
The Elves and the Shoemaker
ISBN 978 0 7496 8543 0
The Ugly Duckling
ISBN 978 0 7496 8544 7
Sleeping Beauty
ISBN 978 0 7496 8545 4
The Frog Prince
ISBN 978 0 7496 8546 1
The Princess and the Pea
ISBN 978 0 7496 8547 8
Dick Whittington
ISBN 978 0 7496 8548 5
Cinderella
ISBN 978 0 7496 7417 5
Snow White
ISBN 978 0 7496 7418 2
The Pied Piper of Hamelin
ISBN 978 0 7496 7419 9
Jack and the Beanstalk
ISBN 978 0 7496 7422 9
The Three Billy Goats Gruff
ISBN 978 0 7496 7420 5
The Emperor's New Clothes
ISBN 978 0 7496 7421 2

For more Hopscotch books go to:
www.franklinwatts.co.uk

*hardback

Daisy Dawson

and the
Big Freeze

Other Racing Reads:

Daisy Dawson
by Steve Voake

Daisy Dawson and the Secret Pool
by Steve Voake

Flotsam and Jetsam
by Tanya Landman

Flotsam and Jetsam and the Stormy Surprise
by Tanya Landman

Big Dog Bonnie
by Bel Mooney

Best Dog Bonnie
by Bel Mooney

Anna Hibiscus
by Atinuke

Hooray for Anna Hibiscus!
by Atinuke